Clifford
Sees America

To Dashiell Winslow del Barco and Serena Guissani
—N.B.

The author thanks Frank Rocco and Grace Maccarone for their contributions to this book.

ISBN 978-0-545-23144-2

15 14 13   17 18 19/0

Printed in the U.S.A. 40

First printing, February 2012

Clifford
Sees America

Norman Bridwell

SCHOLASTIC INC.

Emily Elizabeth's parents pack up the ca
The family is going on a trip.

Clifford can't go.

He is sad to say good-bye to Emily Elizabe

The family drives away.

Just then, the car breaks down.

"Oh, no," says Dad.

"Oh, no," says Emily Elizabeth.

The family goes back home.

"I have an idea," says Emily Elizabeth.
Everyone is happy.

Clifford takes the family to New York City. Look at the signs!

When they leave, they say good-bye
to the big green lady.

Clifford runs and runs until
he sees an old bell.

Oops!
Did Clifford break the bell?

The man says not to worry.
The bell already had that crack.

Clifford hits the road again.
Where are all the people going?

It's a car race!
Clifford wants to race, too!

He wins!

Clifford runs off the track.
He comes to a river.

It is big.
But not too big for Clifford.

Clifford runs north.

The family sees four big heads.

Clifford likes them.

Everyone on the road is friendly.

"Look!" says Emily Elizabeth.
Clifford has never seen water like this!

"Don't get too close," she says.
"That water is hot!"

The family comes to a city with hills
and winding streets.
Clifford loves sliding down.

Now they are at the ocean.
They can't see it
because of the fog.

But they can hear a boat
blowing its foghorn.
It may be in trouble.

Another foghorn blows.
There are two boats.
They are going to crash!

Clifford dives in.

He can't swim fast enough.

Clifford huffs and puffs.

He blows the fog away.
The boats can see each other.

Hooray for Clifford!
It's the best vacation ever!